Top 10 Romance of 2012, 2015, and 2016.

— BOOKLIST: THE NIGHT IS MINE,
HOT POINT, HEART STRIKE

One of our favorite authors.

— RT BOOK REVIEWS

Buchman has catapulted his way to the top tier
of my favorite authors.

— FRESH FICTION

A favorite author of mine. I'll read anything that
carries his name, no questions asked. Meet your
new favorite author!

— THE SASSY BOOKSTER, FLASH OF
FIRE

M.L. Buchman is guaranteed to get me lost in a
good story.

— THE READING CAFE, WAY OF THE
WARRIOR: NSDQ

I love Buchman's writing. His vivid descriptions bring everything to life in an unforgettable way.

— PURE JONEL, HOT POINT

EMILY'S CHRISTMAS GIFT

A HENDERSON'S RANCH BIG SKY STORY

M. L. BUCHMAN

Buchman Bookworks

SIGN UP FOR M. L. BUCHMAN'S
NEWSLETTER TODAY

and receive:
Release News
Free Short Stories
a Free book

Do it today. Do it now.
http://free-book.mlbuchman.com

Other works by M. L. Buchman:

The Night Stalkers
MAIN FLIGHT
The Night Is Mine
I Own the Dawn
Wait Until Dark
Take Over at Midnight
Light Up the Night
Bring On the Dusk
By Break of Day
WHITE HOUSE HOLIDAY
Daniel's Christmas
Frank's Independence Day
Peter's Christmas
Zachary's Christmas
Roy's Independence Day
Damien's Christmas
AND THE NAVY
Christmas at Steel Beach
Christmas at Peleliu Cove
5E
Target of the Heart
Target Lock on Love
Target of Mine

Firehawks
MAIN FLIGHT
Pure Heat
Full Blaze
Hot Point
Flash of Fire
Wild Fire
SMOKEJUMPERS
Wildfire at Dawn
Wildfire at Larch Creek
Wildfire on the Skagit

Delta Force
Target Engaged
Heart Strike
Wild Justice

White House Protection Force
Off the Leash
On Your Mark
In the Weeds

Where Dreams
Where Dreams are Born
Where Dreams Reside
Where Dreams Are of Christmas
Where Dreams Unfold
Where Dreams Are Written

Eagle Cove
Return to Eagle Cove
Recipe for Eagle Cove
Longing for Eagle Cove
Keepsake for Eagle Cove

Henderson's Ranch
Nathan's Big Sky
Big Sky, Loyal Heart

Love Abroad
Heart of the Cotswolds: England
Path of Love: Cinque Terre, Italy

Dead Chef Thrillers
Swap Out!
One Chef!
Two Chef!

Deities Anonymous
Cookbook from Hell: Reheated
Saviors 101

SF/F Titles
The Nara Reaction
Monk's Maze
the Me and Elsie Chronicles

Strategies for Success (NF)
Managing Your Inner Artist/Writer
Estate Planning for Authors

CHAPTER 1

*E*mily watched Mark being as calm as could be and tried not to resent it. When the heavy Montana snowstorms of December kept them indoors at the main ranch house, he was content to slouch low on the couch and watch a Disney movie with the girls in the cozy family area off the kitchen.

If they wanted to build a fort—Emily always thought of it as a fort, though the girls kept insisting they were tents—Mark would reconfigure the family sitting area off the kitchen no matter what inconvenience it caused the adults.

Between the three of them, they made sure that each construction looked unlike any prior effort. A tropical paradise one time, decorated mostly with one of the ranch hand's awful Hawaiian shirt collection. Another time, a Cheyenne teepee built with Mark's mother's lovely weavings. She'd particularly liked that one. Being in Montana, and especially if Julie was around to help, Western themes were common, often with horse tack or some of her rodeo trophies for decoration.

In the summers Mark lived to fly tourists around in his helicopter and fish, but in the winter his one joy was keeping his girls happy.

That she herself was one of "his girls" always made their daughters giggle with delight. And she *was* happy. All she had to do was watch her daughters and she let their constantly bubbling joy wash over her. They might build their forts—*tents* with their father. But it was never considered complete until she had joined them for the final tour. Mark often left some final task for her to do so that she'd at least feel included. Then they would all lie in it together—Mark at the center with all three of "his girls" clinging happily to him.

Those were the best moments of her life. Perhaps a close second to waking in his arms on the long quiet winter mornings before Tessa and Belle sprang to life like a pair of Jill-in-the-boxes.

She'd known he was a good man and a great commander, but his daughters had never met "The Viper" who used to scare the shit out of everybody, including her. His steel gray eyes had rarely been revealed from behind his mirrored shades. He'd even proposed to her while wearing them—after dark. Which was perhaps the only thing that had kept her from turning into a complete empty-headed mush in that moment.

But his daughters only saw the sky gray that his eyes shone when he was happiest—and the mirrored shades were now worn only in the strong Montana sun. It was impossible for her *not* be happy while she watched the stern, taciturn, demanding Major Mark "The Viper" Henderson (retired) have no compunction about acting as the total goofball with his girls. He was a better father than she was a mother, but she didn't know what to do about that. When they were upset, it was her they came to, so she still had something. But it often meant she got the tears and Mark earned all the cheers.

Emily didn't resent it…much. She mostly just wished it was somehow different.

She turned to the fire and watched what she could see of the flames. They were partially blocked by a great bulge in this week's fort, which was huge by any previous standard.

This room was where the family lived during the day when they weren't out on the ranch. The high-timbered main room and the dining room with its forty-person pine table was for the guests. In the long, bitter, off-season months, it was also where all the locals gathered for the occasional party to break the monotony of winter.

That was for others. The family lived in the kitchen. The kitchen itself was a full commercial setup, decorated like in ranch-house warm timber and cool granite stone. At the near end stood a large plank table of Douglas fir where the family and the ranch hands ate their meals together.

This sitting area to the side had a big stone fireplace, and a scattering of couches and armchairs enough for the entire staff…or there had been until the kids started showing up. Once they graduated from lap-sized, they would have to squeeze in some more furniture. The bookcases that lined the river stone walls already had more shelves added to accommodate the girls' picture books.

Of course more furniture couldn't happen with their latest fort in place—she could only see half the fire from her favorite end of the couch.

It was like a mighty Christmas igloo, its walls built high with pillows raided from all of the guest cabins that were closed for the winter. Mark had waded out into the freezing dawn this morning to cut down and drag home a ten-foot larch to stand at its center. Now, with the tree up and their pillow-wall built, the three of them were madly working away inside. Only the tree's single uppermost branch was visible above the domed roof, like a wide smoke hole escaping the dome of pillows.

Whenever there was a newborn about, either Chelsea's or Julie's boy, their father was instantly abandoned without further thought—which made her feel a little better. Of course, then Emily had to keep a close eye so that the girls didn't smother the two infants with affection. How in the world she'd raised two such...*girls* was a mystery to her. At five, Tessa was an utter extrovert who had all the ranch hands completely wrapped around her tiny pinkie. Belle at three was the steadier one, but only by comparison.

Emily didn't pace when the heavy snow and the biting cold winds forced them to remain indoors, but she wished she'd taken up watching sports on television or something. But after a career of flying helicopters first to war and then to wildfire, watching a bunch of guys chase a football up and down a chunk of AstroTurf in little one- and two-yard spurts couldn't be called exciting.

"I'm absolutely hiring Mark for the next seventeen years," Chelsea plummeted down into the big armchair beside Emily's end of the couch, then had to drag her fingers through her long hair to toss it over her shoulder so she could see. Her cheeks were brilliant red after crossing the snow from where she and her husband, the ranch manager, lived on the other side of the barnyard. Maybe Emily should grow her gold-blonde hair as long, the way Mark kept hinting, but it had been chopped dead straight to her shoulders for her entire life.

Emily saw Mark now sitting on the braided rug with Chelsea's three-month old boy Christopher cradled in his arms—whose hair was already as red as his mother's. Tessa and Belle were leaning on his thighs from either side and reaching over to inspect the infant who watched with such wide, serious eyes. Her own fair hair hadn't been passed on to either daughter, having no chance against Mark's genes from his brown-haired father and Cheyenne mother.

"Or maybe I'll just knock you off and get two husbands, keep Doug for me and have Mark for the kid." Chelsea extended her feet toward the fire.

"I'm notoriously hard to kill." Emily's specialty had been black-in-black missions. Black ops so sensitive that they were talked about with no one, ever. And so dangerous that each one was a curse of its own. Mark accompanied her on or referred vaguely to four—she'd stopped counting as she neared ten.

"Oh, don't worry, Emily," Chelsea slouched lower. "I'd like, uh, get Julie to do it for me. She was raised a cowgirl and knows how to do the icky stuff."

"I'm a horsegirl now. And do what?" Julie settled very slowly on the couch beside Emily, careful not to wake Jared asleep in her arms. Like her own children, Jared had his father's dark hair and eyes rather than Julia's wheat blonde and blue. If he'd slept through the snowy trek down the hill from their cabin, then it would take far more than a small bump to wake him, but Emily knew better than to say such a thing to a new mother. She had to smile at her own worries about Tessa in the beginning.

She did scoop up Jared and hold him while Julie shed her thick coat and tossed it over a maple wood chair. Then she settled back on the plaid sofa and took Jared back, again with infinite care.

Like the toddler-magnets they were, Tessa and Belle appeared on either side of Julie. Tessa sat on Julie's far side, but Belle pushed and squirmed—with plenty of bumps that Jared never noticed—until she was sitting between Emily and Julie. Emily looped an arm around her daughter, not as if there was anywhere else to put it, and kissed her on top of the head.

"I need you to...uh," Chelsea glanced at the two young girls before answering Julie, "...*remove* Emily for me. Kinda permanently so I can have Mark as a full-time babysitter."

"Too late," Julie gently blocked Belle reaching over to wake Jared. Belle was completely enamored of Jared's big eyes and the two of them could stare at each other for hours. "I've already got dibs. Besides, I thought we liked Emily?"

"We do. But where has that gotten us?"

"They grow, you know," Emily decided it was time for a subject change to something other than her demise. "Far too quickly, I might add." She pulled one of Ama's Cheyenne blankets off the back of the couch —this one she'd loved from the first moment, so rich with warm golds and dark reds in a geometric pattern. Spreading it over Julie's and the girls' laps earned her contented smiles.

"See?" Julie looked over at Chelsea. "She knows things. I vote that we keep her."

"Well, she is out there ahead of us," Chelsea finally agreed. "So, what are the good bits waiting for us?"

"We're almost done with diapers."

"Oh God," the two women moaned in unison. "Can't happen too soon."

"Thankfully, Mark is okay trading off on that duty."

"That does it," Chelsea declared. "Sorry, Emily. We really like you, but you're *totally* toast."

"I've still got dibs on Mark." The threat didn't seem too serious as Julie was looking down at her sleeping son with a big smile on her face.

Mark was bent halfway over from placing the now-sleeping Christopher into Chelsea's arms when he finally clued into the last comment. He paused, inspecting all of them carefully.

"Why does this sound like a conversation I want no part of?"

"Because you are a very smart man who loves his wife above any other woman on Earth."

"It's true," Mark shrugged happily before stepping around the back of the couch and leaning down to kiss her from the side.

Emily could feel her internal compass slowly returning to True North. It wasn't often she flew off course, but with Mark's lips on hers, she managed to rediscover her rudder control.

"Oh man," Chelsea groaned in envy.

"Chelsea's right," Julie agreed. "You'd better watch your back, Emily. We're ganging up on you and you're going down. Soon."

"By Christmas."

Emily ignored them both as Mark drew out the kiss to tease them. No complaints from her.

"Where are *your* men?" Mark asked when he finally let her surface for air, leaving her heartrate up about Black Hawk rotor speed. "Two such beautiful women with babies in their arms shouldn't be sitting here unkissed."

"They abandoned us."

"Left us destitute."

"They may have mumbled something about feeding the horses."

"So here we sit."

"In our prime."

"Unkissed," they finished in unison and both aimed ridiculous puckers at Mark and batted their eyelashes. Well, Chelsea did. Julie tried but mostly looked down and blushed for being so forward.

"Feeding the horses, huh? I'd better go check on them." He didn't leave at a run, but he definitely used his best ground-eating stride.

"Ooo," Chelsea cooed loudly. "Looks good from behind too. All mine."

Mark double-timed it out as the three of them shared a laugh.

When he was gone, there was a long silence. Long enough for Belle to slip into a nap against Emily's side and for Tessa to yawn broadly before curling up at the end of the sofa and resting her head on Julie's thigh while Jared wrapped his tiny hand around her pinkie without quite waking.

"What's up with you, Emily?" Julie asked softly.

"There's something up with you?" Chelsea peered at her in surprise.

"Nothing." Emily ignored the slump that Mark had only temporarily lifted. She toyed with the blanket's fringe for a moment before she caught herself at it and tucked her hands out of sight. "Besides, since when can either of you tell what I'm thinking?"

"Since forever. We're your best friends," Julie spoke softly.

"Yeah. Maybe we aren't all experienced and old like you, but we know shit."

They'd both found the love of their life and reproduced in their early twenties. It had taken her until thirty to find love, then more years of service, finally the first kid…and that had been five years ago. Forty wasn't here yet, but it was incoming—fast. She closed her eyes.

This was December. She'd been born in… Yep, really fast.

"Is forty bumming you out?"

Emily sat with it for a while. "No, I don't think that's it…"

"Told you something was up with her," Julie whispered to Chelsea.

"Of course, you two youngsters are enough to make a grown woman a little nuts."

"But you love us both anyway, huh?"

Emily looked at Chelsea and couldn't deny that truth.

"Like daughters?" Julie's voice was slightly wistful. Her family life hadn't been real fun. Just the hard life of a cattle ranch with a strict father, a silent mother, and three older brothers, but none of the joy she'd discovered when she'd fallen in love with the man who was now Henderson's Ranch's head chef.

"*Daughters?*" Emily winced. "Now you're just *trying* to make me feel old. How about younger sisters?"

Julie actually nodded fiercely. As if it was important.

Chelsea too was blinking hard. "If I wasn't afraid of waking this little terror, I'd come over there and give you major kiss."

Curiously, Emily caught herself in mid-sniffle, but managed to take a deep breath to cover it.

"It's just,,," She honestly didn't know.

"Pre-Christmas blues?"

"Year-end blahs?"

"Desperate need for a third child?"

That earned them a bark of laughter that made all four children stir in their sleep.

They all held their breaths until the kids had resettled and the only sounds were the fierce Montana winds struggling vainly to rattle the solid house.

"Not a chance," Emily kept her voice low just in case they weren't fully asleep again. "I don't think Mark would mind, but having your kids late means all sorts of strange things. I'll be sixty before this one graduates from college." She could feel Belle so warm and safe against her side. What would it be like when Belle was a woman grown like Julie or Chelsea and maybe with a child of her own? Out in the world where Emily couldn't protect her?

At Tessa's age, she herself had already had a crush on Peter Matthews—the perfect older boy next door. But he'd married and become President of the United States. She'd gone to West Point and become the first woman of the Night Stalkers. By Julie and Chelsea's age, she'd been flying helicopters on her second tour into war zones with the 101st Airborne.

"Sixty? Shit, you *are* old, sis."

"Go to hell, Chelsea."

"Not gonna happen. I've got you for a big sister, means I've gotta being doing something right."

Emily knew Chelsea had earned a laugh, but she couldn't seem to find it. She lay her head back on the couch and wondered what was wrong with her. Maybe it *was* just the season. Or that Night Stalkers helicopter pilots, unlike most Special Operations Forces, could fly well into their fifties—if they hadn't reproduced. It wasn't some rule that had kept her out. Instead, her own fears for her child's safety had cost her that finely-honed *edge* that made a true Spec Ops pilot. Maybe it was that...

Something was wrong, and she had no idea what.

She heard a soft gasp from Chelsea that made her open her eyes.

And looked up directly into Peter's. Mark and Peter were grinning at her—upside down over the back of the soft, brown-leather couch.

"Surprise, Squirt."

"You're supposed to be in Washington, D.C., Sneaker Boy." Her childhood nickname for the former President of the United States. Except he wasn't anymore. He was the Secretary of State. His nickname was still Sneaker Boy.

She heard a deep, guffaw in the background.

"Hi, Frank."

"Good afternoon, Major Beale," the head of Peter's Secret Service Protection Detail sounded as formal as ever. Yet another reminder of what she'd left behind.

Then she looked over at Mark.

"You seemed kinda down, Emily. So I invited Peter out for Christmas as a surprise. His wife, kid, and maybe a few others will be out next week."

"You're feeling down?" Peter suddenly sounded worried. Just exactly what she didn't need—the Secretary of State and former President flying to Montana in the middle of winter to hover. There'd be no point trying to explain it to Mark; he'd never be convinced he'd overreacted.

"You're what?" "What's wrong?" Apparently done with the horses, Chelsea's and Julie's husbands chimed in from somewhere out of view.

Emily sat up and looked at her younger sisters. "Don't bother killing me, just take Mark for yourselves, please. Now."

"Do you really change diapers?" Chelsea turned to Mark, who shrugged a yes.

"Dibs," Julie said again.

CHAPTER 2

"*S*eriously, Em. What's wrong?"

She'd led Peter through the bitter cold out to the horse barn, because no matter what Mark thought, the Secretary of State didn't fly to Montana just because a friend was feeling sad. Though she had to give Mark a few points for noticing how she *was* feeling when she'd barely realized it herself.

She stopped at Chesapeake's stall. The barn was warm with the scent of horse and hay. The light was dim beneath the blowing storm, making it feel almost as cozy as the kitchen—as long as you were wearing a jacket or a horse blanket.

She hadn't had the clarity of mind to remember to grab a treat from the house, but Chelsea kept a bag of carrots in her office and Emily had grabbed one as she walked by.

Breaking off a piece, she palmed it to her horse. The big chestnut mare lipped it off her palm and crunched it down. She leaned her cheek against the horse's and felt her chew.

"Mark's right. You are looking down."

"Which isn't why you're here."

"Well, not all of it, but—"

"Why are you here, Sneaker Boy?"

Peter laughed, then startled when Julie's black-and-white painted horse, Clarence, stuck his head out of his stall to see what was going on and almost knocked Peter over.

Emily gave him a chunk of Chesapeake's carrot as a reward.

"I don't know as I'd have come for either reason separately, but when Mark called to invite me out and…" he shrugged. "It's about Dilya."

She spun to face him, but he only looked concerned, not afraid.

"What about her?" Emily barely managed to keep her voice steady. Dilya was the war-orphan adopted daughter of her best friend Archie and his wife Kee, the first woman to qualify for the Night Stalkers after she herself had. That terrified and starved ten-year-old was now a lovely seventeen-year-old, living in the White House as nanny to the First and Second children.

"She's…" Peter's face showed that he really didn't know as he stumbled to a halt.

"Okay. Not sick. Not in trouble. What?"

Peter finally shrugged. "She reminds me too much of you."

"Of me?" She showed him how to hold some carrot

to feed to Clarence before she fed the greens to Chesapeake. Why on earth would that be?

"Remember when we first met?"

"No. I think I was about three days old. My memory is good, but even I have limits."

"I mean when we re-met."

"You mean when I slammed the head of your Protection Detail onto his ass on the White House's main staircase?" She raised her voice enough to make sure Frank Adams could hear her as he returned from checking that there were no four-legged assassins lurking in the horse barn.

"Are we really back to this, Major? You just gotta keep bringing that up, don't you?"

"It *was* memorable."

Frank grumbled as he moved by to check the other end of the barn.

"Yes," Peter waited until Frank was again out of earshot. "I'd been following your career for some time by then. And I was horrified at the dangers you were going into."

"Because I was a woman."

Peter looked down and scuffed one of his perfect leather shoes at the dirty straw. For all his supposed sophistication, he was still a guy—which meant she'd never understand him.

"That," he admitted, "and because you were my friend. You were the little girl next door who was suddenly flying thirty-million-dollar helicopters straight into harm's way."

"What has this got to do with Dilya?"

17

"You know that girl's nose for trouble?"

"You don't know the half of it." In her first month after they'd rescued her, Dilya had identified two men so intent on revenge that they didn't care if it could start the next World War. Then she'd stowed away on a clandestine insertion deep into Uzbekistan to stop them. A detail that was never included in any action report.

"And I'm guessing I don't want to. But now? I'm getting worried for her, Em."

Emily glanced up at her secure office within the stable. Her Tac Room (short for Tactical) had been built directly over the Tack Room (filled with saddles and bridles). It had been finished with the same, aged wood, so that it didn't stand out at all. Its windows were dark—with special glass that appeared opaque even when lit from within. The only clue from the outside that it was anything special was the very sophisticated lock mounted out of sight from below. From there, at Peter's behest, she'd created the White House Protection Force. The WHPF had proven to be immensely successful, saving the new President's life on three separate occasions and averting any number of other minor disasters.

And despite Emily's best intentions, Dilya had several times ended up far too close to the action for comfort. The last time, nearly being shot down over Canadian soil.

"So, what do you want me to do? Scare her straight?"

She could see Peter's face brighten.

"You know that's not going to happen, don't you?"

And he looked worried again.

"She's an incredibly bright kid. And she's grown up with the elite Night Stalkers company for companions, a sniper mother, a strategic consultant father, and essentially unlimited access to your and now Zachary's White House. You think she was just being cute all those times she 'hung out' in the Oval with you? I guarantee you that Dilya was never an innocent child—at least not since we found her. Watching both your parents be executed right in front of you will do that to a kid."

Peter leaned sadly against the stall door. His idea of casual was a two-piece suit rather than a three-piece under his heavy black wool coat. Clarence snorted in his ear and made him jump away in alarm. Out of carrot, she made a point of scritching the horse's cheek with her fingers until he huffed out a happy sigh.

"If we can't keep her out of trouble, how do we teach her to judge when she's in too deep or at least to cry for help?"

Emily leaned back against Chesapeake's neck. Her childhood friend had been Peter, who was six years older than she was. Julie had been right, Emily knew things because she was out ahead of them…but Belle was two and Tessa was five. That wasn't seventeen. She knew nothing yet about anything after age five. Her only solution had been to treat Dilya as a small adult…one who wasn't so small anymore.

But it was a crucial question. Peter was right, Dilya's well-being depended on it. And she knew just who to ask.

CHAPTER 3

*C*onvincing Peter that there were some things he didn't want to know had proved just as hard as usual, but Emily had practice at it. With Frank's help, she soon had him shooed back over to the main house.

Mounting the stairs to her Tac Room, she keycoded the door, offered her eye for retinal scan, then locked the door behind her.

The one-way glass gave her a long view of the horse stalls, their occupants lazing through the cold winter day, happily napping and munching on hay. Chelsea came into the barn at the far end of the stalls. She waved up as she always did in case Emily was watching, and headed into her own office. As the ranch's horse manager, she was meticulous in the care of her charges and the recent vet's visit to give all of them a checkup had probably left a pile of paperwork.

Emily liked the company when they were both working out here, even if they were isolated in separate offices. Chelsea didn't have the security clearance to ever be inside this room.

Emily had already done her check of the public world news this morning. Now, in her secure space, she flipped through today's briefing documents from the various agencies. No real surprises—hot spots were still hot, but nothing abnormal. She'd be paged if there was a real crisis calling for her attention, but it wasn't the sort of day where that seemed likely. The First and Second families were having their typical White House workdays without travel. Which also meant Dilya would be rattling around the White House.

She tapped in a coded signal and settled in to wait while she read up on that latest internal status reports from NATO.

Her Tac Room assistant, Lauren, had proved herself immensely capable when dealing with military contacts. But the other side of Emily's information network—the one that reached deep into the White House itself—no one knew about except herself. With Lauren honeymooning at Disneyland over the holidays, Emily didn't have to worry about shooing her out to place this call.

"Hello, my dear." Her central screen lit with the face of one of the White House Protection Force's primary assets. Her gray hair framed an ageless face. Sometimes it seemed she'd aged past old crone and gone straight on to wizened. At other times, her face was clear enough that the gray hair was a shock. Today, she simply appeared what she was—a beautiful woman in her seventies (probably).

Behind her ranged the most unusual library in Washington, DC—which was saying something. Emily knew from her one visit there that it wasn't large. Her office felt even smaller because every inch of wall space from floor to ceiling was packed solid with books. Also on display were some of the more clandestine tools of the spy trade, which the shadows hadn't afforded her a chance to study. It was also perhaps the most accurate library on spies and spy craft ever assembled. There were less than a dozen people who knew where it lay— behind the door of Room 043-Mechanical in the White House Residence's deepest subbasement. And the woman in charge had been one of the greatest spies, including undocumented ones, of them all.

A blurred red-and-green glow stood to one side of the camera's view—too close to be clearly seen. A desktop Christmas tree perhaps? What did a master spy's Christmas tree look like? Probably a cone of stacked red-and-green code books used over the last half-century.

"Hello, Miss Watson. How are you today?"

"Oh, I'm good my dear. Very good. Thank you for asking. Is there something amiss that I'm unaware of?"

"Not likely," Emily sometimes wondered if Miss Watson was helping her keep the White House safe or if she was helping Miss Watson.

Miss Watson offered one of her grandmotherly smiles, "I don't know that you've ever made a social call before."

And at Emily's wince, Miss Watson clearly understood that this one wasn't either.

It wasn't that she didn't want to, it was that she never thought to. Not a single one of those fine skills that her mother, one of DC social queens, had struggled to cultivate in her only offspring had stuck.

"Emily, dear child…"

She almost laughed. She now had two younger "sisters" and all of them had children, yet—

"Tell me the reason you called, then we can talk about why you should have called earlier."

Emily tried looking at the books behind Miss Watson. Was there a guide to mindreading tucked away somewhere on those shelves? Unsure quite what Miss Watson meant, she described Peter's concerns about Dilya.

"That child was never young. Such potential."

Emily suddenly wasn't sure that Miss Watson's influence on Dilya was a good thing. What little she knew of Miss Watson's exploits told of the immense risks a woman could take in the name of the Cold War. It had been inevitable that Dilya's natural inquisitiveness had brought them together. Unfortunately what happened at the White House was outside of her control. Emily could protect, but she couldn't control.

Instead, her skill had always been in locating and cultivating exceptional talent. The President's new driver, one of his dog handlers, and others she'd helped put in place kept the President safer far beyond anything the Secret Service would understand—or ever be told about.

The White House Protection Force did *not* include Dilya, and yet she seemed to end up in the center of every problem—even when those problems became life-threatening.

"The girl is so independent. Perhaps too much so."

"Too much?" Emily had always prided herself on her own independence. It was what had let her succeed in a male world—absolute self-reliance.

"Yes. She knows a great deal more about depending solely on her own judgment than even you, my dear child. Despite your deservedly decorated career. And don't we both know about some of the decorations you can never admit to."

Emily kept her best neutral expression on her face, but Miss Watson merely winked. No one, but *no one* other than the former President and the Joint Chiefs of Staff should know about her medals from black-in-black operations. Even Mark didn't know about those. No more than he'd know that she was technically still on active duty as a consultant.

"Dilya has carefully positioned herself to know more than everyone around her here at the White House," Miss Watson continued blithely. "I even hold a hope that someday she— Well, never mind that now. I believe that you've raised a valid question and I shall give it some thought. It is Christmas soon. Perhaps I shall give her a Christmas gift after all."

Emily considered what that might mean and suddenly wished she hadn't placed this call in the first place. Perhaps she should call Dilya and warn her away from Miss Watson. Actually, she could think of no faster way to drive Dilya directly into the fray. In that, she and Dilya were much alike.

Before Emily could open her mouth to protest or perhaps even try to call Miss Watson off, she continued so smoothly that Emily never managed a word.

"Now, my dear. Let's talk about what's troubling you."

"Nothing's troubling me."

"It isn't age," Miss Watson ignored her fib. "No woman as beautiful as you with two lovely children and such an exceptional husband can doubt that she is in the prime of her life."

She sighed.

"And I must compliment you on the fine job you did helping your husband transition to retired life. You are much better with people than you think you are. You picture yourself so austere and remote, yet people are drawn to you anyway."

Emily opened her mouth to protest, then closed it. She *had* just acquired two younger sisters this morning. Miss Watson couldn't know about them, could she? At least not yet? But she was right, the emotions on their faces had been no lie. Emily had always built team loyalty by being the best—no matter what it cost her. By being the best, she'd attracted the best. Yet it wasn't by outperforming anyone on the team that Julie had asked, *I thought we liked Emily?* And Chelsea had agreed, *We really do.*

"I remember such a time of reflection shortly before I died."

"You…died?"

"Oh yes, dear. Any number of times." She nudged a finger against the Christmas tree that was just a blur on the edge of the screen. It moved, so it wasn't books. Maybe it was better if she didn't know. "It is an easy way to cover your tracks in an on-going operation. But I'm referring to when I let the CIA believe I had died."

"How did they take it?"

"Oh, it was a lovely funeral. I have a star up on their wall, which is quite an honor in my business."

"And they still don't know about you surviving?"

Miss Watson shrugged, "There comes a time in a woman's life where one must move closer to the heart. We aren't men, after all."

Emily felt that was rather obvious.

"You'll want to think about that, child. You are a woman grown. You've fought for the right, and done the duties that a man does. For great achievers like us, struggling within a society not ready for us, we must now come to terms with being...ourselves."

"How did you do it?"

But Miss Watson's ghost of a smile demurred.

How had she done it? From what little Emily knew, Miss Watson might have always been in the White House subbasement. Yet apparently she'd also been a spy in the final years of the Vietnam War and had a Soviet two-star general as a lover. Emily, too, heard things.

She'd first met Miss Watson years before during her brief residence at the White House as the First Lady's personal chef. She'd thought nothing of it at the time— some elderly White House staffer she'd chatted with about the war she was fighting in Afghanistan. In hindsight Emily could see that things had changed for her from that moment. She'd— "Oh, I became *your* weapon."

Miss Watson offered her a slightly surprised expression.

"All those additional black-in-black ops. The toughest missions—"

"—Came to you because of your supreme confidence and exceptional abilities. Don't try to make me the wizard behind the curtain of your career, Emily. You are tactically an exceptional woman. It is the bigger picture that slips by you. Dilya is beginning to see her own bigger picture, which is why you worry about her— we fear what we don't understand."

"But—"

"Oh, my dear child," Miss Watson was gently shaking her head. "In the later years, you are still *yourself.* But the challenges are new. You must learn who you, yourself are. Rediscover or, if that fails, discover for the first time, the amazing woman you are."

"That's your advice?"

"The voice of experience."

Emily couldn't help but remember Julie leaning forward just this morning, *She knows things. I vote that we keep her.*

Man oh man, did she ever have them fooled.

"What did you—"

"Oh no, child. It would be cheating to tell. Besides, Dilya is far more my daughter than you are—at least in how she thinks. You must discover your own woman."

"Why doesn't that feel helpful?"

"Because you're still thinking as if you live in a

man's world, challenging the status quo." Then Miss Watson shook herself lightly, glanced at her bookshelves somewhere out of sight, and suddenly appeared much older.

"Miss Watson, are you—"

"It is time I sent for Dilya."

"Miss Watson?" Emily could think of nothing else to say.

"Go see your family, dear." Then she was gone.

Emily sat in her small Tac Room and looked at blank screen, she tried not to feel sadder than before the call. Did the poor woman even have any family? Did she even have someone to spend Christmas with? Not that Emily knew of, and yet here she was dumping her own doubts upon Miss Watson.

She knew she could trust Dilya to Miss Watson's care and she'd hear soon enough what had happened. Emily had forgotten how much she liked Miss Watson and promised herself that her next call would be strictly social. Or when she needed a break from the Montana winter, she'd visit her parents in DC and arrange to drop in on the White House subbasement personally.

As for herself, none of it felt like a solution to anything.

CHAPTER 4

"What are you up to, babe?" Mark slid down on the couch beside her. He flipped up the edge of the big Cheyenne weaving she'd thrown over herself hours before while she'd watched the fire burn. There were only a few embers left, dying from lack of tending.

"What time is it?"

"Way early, but I missed you in bed." He pulled her into his arms and kissed her on the temple.

A week had passed and she was no closer to understanding any of Miss Watson's life lessons. Now she was out of time and simply had to shake it off.

Later today the ranch house would become much more lively. Vice President Daniel Darlington and his family had decided to fly out for Christmas along with Peter's wife and child. The local ranchers' potluck was going to get a big surprise tonight—for security's sake, no one would be warned ahead of time. Of course surprises were fair on both sides of the coin—she also hadn't forewarned the Secret Service just how many rifles would arrive tonight, hanging in the back windows of Montana pickup trucks.

The girls' pillow igloo fort would have to come down —or it should. Knowing she'd lose that battle, she decided to leave well enough alone. Julie's husband Nathan and Mark's mom Ama would be awake soon and the three of them were planning to cook throughout the day. All week, Peter had practically taken over her secure Tac Room in the barn, doing Secretary of State things, so at least he'd been out from underfoot.

With the ease of long practice, Mark had eased her into his lap with her barely noticing until her head lay on his shoulder and his hand cradled her behind underneath the warm blanket.

"This isn't like you, Emily. Got me worried some." She'd always enjoyed feeling the deep rumble in his chest when he spoke.

"That makes two of us."

"You missing the action?"

She shook her head. At first the adrenaline-junkie withdrawal had been hard, but she'd expected that. Besides, she hadn't gone straight from Spec Ops to civilian—the years flying to wildfire and her occasional calls to consult had eased the transition.

"Sick of the cooking?"

No. She loved that. Mark's mother Ama had run the kitchen for over a decade, but cooked much less now. Nathan, a world-class chef who'd stumbled into love with Julie, had taken over the kitchen with such zeal that

Emily could come play whenever the mood struck her, but she didn't have to worry when it didn't.

"Nothing about the kids?"

"I couldn't love Belle and Tessa more if they were part of me."

"They *were* part of you."

"Exactly my point."

As if on cue, the two girls appeared, still rubbing their eyes sleepily. In moments, they were all curled up together under the warm blanket. It was awkward, a little uncomfortable, and amazingly perfect.

"Not...us?" Mark whispered against her ear once the girls were settled. They were huddled under the blanket, mostly on her lap, whispering back and forth.

In answer, she managed to twist around enough to kiss Mark. He made it as thorough and perfect as their very first kiss—and she felt no desire to smash his face into an aircraft carrier's table as she'd done the first time.

"Then what?" Mark asked as she once more lay her head upon his shoulder and tightened her arm around Tessa's waist earning a happy giggle from beneath the big quilt.

For the life of her, she hadn't a clue.

CHAPTER 5

The mayhem had started even sooner than she'd anticipated.

Belle and Tessa, finally coming wide awake under the blanket, had found their father's one ticklish spot and completely undone him. To escape, he'd finally fallen off the couch. Turning it into a roll, he regained his feet and moved over to stoke the fire. The girls knew about not interfering around the flames. By the time she and the girls were dressed, Ama had breakfast on the table. Nathan was eating as he worked, assembling the ingredients for Emily's dry rub on the massive roast they'd planned for the potluck.

Second Lady Alice had arrived with their newborn, and Peter's wife Geneviève brought their little girl. At four, she had all the poise and elegance that her mother embodied and Emily's own daughters completely lacked. Belle and Tessa practically transcended on the spot with the additional playmate. She didn't know if she hoped her girls rubbed off on Adele Gloria—simply to harass Peter—or perhaps the other way round and her own girls might become more comprehensible to her. Either way, kid heaven had taken over much of the floor space in front of the fireplace with Mark often in the fray.

Her mood kept lifting through the day.

She'd never thought of herself as a particularly social or even approachable woman, but there were only so many welcoming hugs and joyous smiles that could be aimed her way before that belief became undeniably foolish.

Thankfully, the storm blew out and all that was left were achingly clear starlit skies and bitter cold. But Montanan ranchers had never yet been stopped by mere cold and soon the house was packed. The local ranchers soon shed their awe of the Washington elite—helped in part by all of the children in their pre-Christmas excitement. As more local children had arrived, they'd strained Tessa's and Belle's "dress up" wardrobe to the limit, but Christmas fairies and elves had abounded.

The big afternoon puppy-pile nap on the kitchen's couch had averted most of the exhaustion meltdowns.

And somehow, through the whole thing, the Christmas igloo fort had survived—no mere "tent" could have made it through the constant stream of children in and out of it. Of all the adults, only Mark had been allowed admittance.

As the evening wound down and the ranchers drifted back home through the chill darkness, the family and Washington guests slowly gathered once more in the kitchen. Chairs and benches were dragged over until everyone was packed in close to the fireplace. Hot cocoa, laced with brandy for the grownups, was served all around.

Emily could only look around the circle in wonder. Julie and Chelsea sat nearby with their husbands and babies. Her childhood friend Peter and his lovely Geneviève sat with her friend Vice President Daniel and his cheery wife. All around the room, there wasn't a person here whose life she hadn't touched, and who hadn't touched hers.

How had she not known this? Why was she just seeing it now?

These were her friends. Her family. Just as surely as the action teams of the Night Stalkers 5th Battalion D Company and the firefighters of Mount Hood Aviation had been her family.

She...belonged.

Is this what Miss Watson had been talking about? That somehow, this was her "woman's" role after having lived in the "man's" world for so many years?

Maybe it was. Maybe—

"I think it's time, girls," Mark called, loudly enough to silence all of the conversations.

With a squeal of delight, they launched to their feet in a mad swirl of excitement and fairy wings. Adele Gloria—Peter's and Geneviève's daughter had devolved only a little under Tessa's influence and Tessa had settled (a little)—was rapidly recruited and the three kids disappeared into the Christmas igloo fort.

"Now it's your turn, honey," Mark rose and held out his hand to her.

Emily was terribly conscious that everyone was watching her as she rose to her feet. She should have gone and locked herself in her Tac Room—nobody would dare to disturb her there. Then she certainly wouldn't be the center of attention.

Once she was on her feet, Mark knelt before her, something he hadn't even done while proposing. What was he—

"Up," he patted his shoulder.

"What?"

He hooked one of her knees and dragged it over his shoulder. "Climb aboard, Emily."

"No. I—" she resisted his attempt to grab her other leg.

"Here, Mommy," Belle came out of the igloo and handed her a package wrapped in Christmas paper before racing back in.

Mark took advantage of her momentary distraction and got her astride his shoulders. Then he stood quickly before she could escape. He faced the Christmas igloo and called out.

"Ready, girls?"

A high chorus of "Yes!" was their answer as she hung onto Mark's forehead with one hand and the wrapped present with the other.

"Go!" Mark roared out like commanding a fleet of weapon-laden helicopters into battle.

The igloo wavered as if hit from the inside. Then it wavered again.

The assembled crowd was absolutely silent in anticipation.

Another impact and one pillow fell off the top of the wall.

Then there was a shout of little girls joining forces in some supreme effort. The three of them, with their arms locked together, burst clean through the side of the pillow igloo, which fell and scattered in every direction.

Emily joined in everyone's gasp of wonder.

The larch tree, that had stood so long in hiding, was revealed. It had been decorated with hand-made ornaments, lights, popcorn-and-cranberry strings, and everything else that little girls and her husband could think of. People were pulling aside the tumbled pillows until a great mound of them had been piled up behind the couch and the tree stood fully revealed.

"It's beautiful," she barely managed a whisper but somehow Mark heard it through all of the applause and general chatter.

"Not finished yet."

"No, it's perfect."

But he stepped up to the tree, giving her the feeling that she was floating along in a helicopter once more. She considered tugging on his ears to see if they acted like rudder controls, or maybe a cyclic to get her down from here. But his big hands were clamped over her thighs, pinning her in place.

"Emily, open your present."

At a loss for what else to do, she unwrapped it as she teetered high in the air. And discovered a golden star.

The bare top of the larch, the only part of the tree that had ever shown above the pillow igloo, was right at eye level. By reaching out as far as she dared, she was just able to slip it onto the top of the tree.

A fresh round of cheers and applause broke out as Mark stepped back and helped her down to the pine floor. The tree was glorious with its wild decorations and brightly colored lights set off by the golden warmth of the fire's flickering glow.

With Mark's arm around her waist, and the girls' hanging on to either side, they all admired the tree.

Or at least Mark and the girls did.

Emily instead heard the joy and the laughter of her friends gathered around her. So many. So true.

"You're my star," Mark whispered—absolutely the romantic one in their relationship.

This right here, this moment was who she *truly* was.

And Emily could feel that gift all the way to her heart.

And don't miss the companion story: Dilya's Christmas Challenge, a White House Protection Force story.

DILYA'S CHRISTMAS CHALLENGE (EXCERPT)

DON'T MISS THIS CHARMING COMPANION STORY.

*M*iss Watson had considered painting a giant spider web on her door. If it wouldn't draw undue attention, she well might have. Room 043-Mechanical in the White House Residence's lowest subbasement had nothing mechanical in it, at least nothing that a building engineer would ever care about. Good cover because the best cover was a bland one.

Her small desk had once belonged to Assistant Secretary of the Treasury, Harry Dexter White, who had run the Silvermaster spy ring for the Soviet Union for years. Her walls were packed with every biography or interview transcript from a spy going back to the early days of the American colonies. The rubbish about The Craft that consumed so much of the CIA's libraries—written by analysts and others even less informed—were not to be found within her four walls. She also kept a number of the more gruesome tools of the trade on display to remind her of just what horrors the human psyche was capable.

But even at her age, a woman wasn't supposed to feel like Moriarty—Sherlock Holmes' greatest opponent —curled "motionless, like a spider in the centre of its web, but that web has a thousand radiations, and he knows well every quiver of each of them."

She rarely left her office anymore, instead listening only to the information that flowed into her domain rather than gathering it. She allowed only a few bits, a very precious few, to flow back out. Maybe she'd paint the spider web in blacklight or some other ink that wouldn't show. But she'd know was there.

It always surprised her when a thread was activated that she hadn't anticipated. When the computer beeped she dropped a stitch in her knitting in surprise—a nice bit of double-sided colorwork scarf recalling a long ago sunset along the shore of the Black Sea.

Assumptions are dangerous, she reminded herself.

She forced herself to pick up the stitch and count to make sure that everything was put to rights before she answered.

"Hello, my dear." Her screen lit to reveal one of her favorite people. Major Emily Beale (retired—at least according to most official records) had a mind that worked so differently from her own. For that reason if no other, Emily would have been very useful to her. But as a force of nature in her own right, the immensely skilled and well-connected woman brought far more assets than most could muster.

However, she should have known a call was coming.

It wasn't unusual for Emily to call from her Montana ranch, but it was strange that she herself had no inkling of what the topic might be.

"Hello, Miss Watson. How are you today?"

"Oh, I'm good my dear. Very good. Thank you for asking. Is there something amiss that I'm unaware of?"

"Not likely."

Miss Watson couldn't quite resist smiling at the compliment. "I don't know that you've ever made a social call before."

Emily's grimace communicated a great deal. It wasn't social, which was disappointing. But she saw in how Emily's eyes shifted to the side, beyond the breadth of the screen she'd be using, that Emily wished it had been. She was such a sweet woman.

"Emily, dear child…" Miss Watson merely said it to herself, but saw Emily react much more strongly than expected.

A laugh?

A hysterical one?

Major Emily Beale was not the sort given to hysterics.

"Tell me the reason you called, then we can talk about why you should have called earlier."

Emily nodded, "I'm worried about Dilya."

Keep reading at fine retailers everywhere.

BIG SKY DOG WHISPERER
(EXCERPT)

THE HEARTWARMING CONCLUSION TO
THE HENDERSON'S RANCH SERIES.

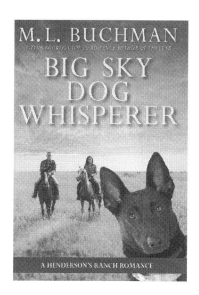

BIG SKY DOG WHISPERER

(EXCERPT)

"This wasn't one of my better ideas."

Nikita's laugh over the phone drove Jodie even deeper under the covers.

"Fine for you. You're still on the inside, Nikita." And Jodie so wasn't. She considered switching her phone to her other ear so that she couldn't hear Nikita's laugh. Holding her phone in her left hand still felt wrong—but the blast that had taken both her and her dog out of action with the SEAL teams had left her right ear completely deaf.

"What made you think that moving back in with your parents made any kind of sense?"

"I like my parents."

"And you don't think that makes you weird?"

"Not being helpful, Nikita." Jodie pulled the covers over her face so that she couldn't see her room. She'd left home at eighteen to go into the Navy. She was back at thirty when twelve years of service was cut off as suddenly as a New York taxi cutting through a crosswalk. Her parents had left her room unchanged over the years so that she'd have somewhere to go when she was on leave.

Everything was familiar, known, safe. Eerily so after a decade in the war zones. Like some part of time had been frozen in this room. The posters on the walls still reflected every band she'd seen at Madison Square Garden as a teen. The shelf above her small desk held every dog book she'd found at used bookstores over the years, starting with *Go, Dog. Go!* and going to Cesar Millan's *Be the Pack Leader* that she'd bought new but never read because she'd joined the Navy a week later. The bed had the blanket that she'd gotten when she was twelve and Nanny had helped her redecorate from a small girl's room to a "grown-up" teen's. They'd gone a little mad at Macy's and she had a carpet the color of a tropical sea, a sunset bedspread, and walls painted in the palest blue of a beachy summer sky.

And here Nikita was, telling her that rather than being embraced by the room she was being *entombed* here —as if that was helpful information.

What better way to ease back into civilian life than sitting at the breakfast table as Mom and Dad prepared for their morning ride into the city? Mom would take the A or C train from Brooklyn to the New York Downtown Hospital where she'd been a nurse since college. Rather than taking the more convenient F train, Dad would ride with her, then stay on up into Midtown. He'd stroll along 42nd, buying a second cup of coffee before reaching his job as a librarian for NY Public Library. For all Jodie knew, that had been their invariable routine since the day they were married and first moved back into Pop Julius' brownstone.

About the time she went to high school, Pop Julius and Nanny had retired to Florida. Mom and Dad hadn't even moved into the big bedroom on the main floor, saving it as the guest bedroom. She, Mom, and Dad still lived on the second floor. The only thing that had changed was that her little brother, instead of living alone on the third floor, now had his wife and two kids up there with him.

"So, what's the problem, Jodie? You know reentry sucks. Everyone says so. Especially for long-timers like us."

Everyone says so. The insider's statement wasn't helping.

Being back in her childhood home might sound weird, but it didn't suck. She'd lost thirty pounds the day she got mustered out—twenty of body armor; five of sidearm, extra ammo, and other survival crap; and the last five to unhunching her shoulders wondering if she'd die today. That last part felt pretty good. Though she still carried a combat knife in her small knapsack, she didn't feel the need for a concealed sidearm. Brooklyn wasn't a bit like Libya or Syria or...

"The problem..." Jodie hated it, because there was no way to fix it here. "The problem is Brandy."

"What's wrong with her?"

What *wasn't* wrong with her was the real question. Jodie could feel the heat against her leg of the pure black Belgian Malinois lying on top of the covers. Brandy was all nerves wrapped up in a bit of dog. Every sound made her twitch. The throaty diesel of a metro bus two blocks over on Smith Street sent a ripple along Brandy's haunches where they pressed against Jodie's calf. A horn honking at the corner of President and Smith was a flinch of shoulders against her thigh. A siren down their quiet residential street—*Shit!* The first one of those had given her war dog a full-blown panic attack.

During their years overseas together, Jodie had heard her dog make any number of sounds. A whimper could be anything from thirst to worry to knowing it would get her some extra attention. There'd been cries of pain—as Jodie pulled glass shards from the dog's footpads or held her while a medic stitched up a bad laceration from tangling with a feral dog and a length of razor wire. Sharp barks of warning, or excitement during play.

Not until Jodie had brought her to New York had Brandy ever made a cry of pure terror. It was the eeriest sound. High pitched. Like an incoming mortar round whistling down on your head that kept building until it was a pure howl. The sound made sense. It was a mortar that had almost taken both their lives, which made the accuracy of Brandy's imitation creepy as hell. Jodie had finally pinned the frantic dog to the carpet, lying on top of her until Brandy had finally calmed.

That she'd woken the entire family, who'd all tried to storm into her bedroom to see what was happening, hadn't helped matters. Brandy, who'd always loved hanging out with her SEAL squad and all the attention it got her, could no longer deal with any kind of crowd.

Jodie wanted to go get a bagel with cream cheese

and lox at Shelsky's. She wanted to bop over to Carroll Park, buy a Nutty Buddy ice cream cone from the cart vendor, and sit on a bench in the May sunshine watching the kids play on the swings. She wanted to take her dog for a run down the length of the Brooklyn Heights Promenade. Hell, she'd even thought about going back to synagogue to see if there were any answers for the devastation and cruelty she'd witnessed overseas.

Instead, they'd spent her first week home cowering in her ten-by-ten bedroom that would soon be stuffy with June's heat. It was already getting that way because of the need to keep the window closed to muffle any street noise. Even her two nieces didn't dare come into the room anymore after Brandy had snapped at them. Twice a day, Jodie forced Brandy outside; but she had to put on a full harness and muzzle, only daring to lead her out when kids were at school or so late at night that no one else was out walking their dog.

Nikita listened with sympathy. As one of the few other women to work with the SEALs, there was some understanding. Even though Nikita had gone all SEAL Team 6 while Jodie stayed with the Navy teams, they'd somehow stayed connected. Loosely, but connected. Out of desperation—this evening had been another bad one for Brandy and she was shaking now in her sleep—Jodie had called her. The two women were SEALs, about all that they had in common.

But PTSD happened to other people, not to people still on the inside, still serving. It was like an infectious disease, rarely discussed, "instant isolation ward" treatment from both active and veteran personnel as if it was a highly contagious plague—worse than being a dweeb.

It wasn't herself. Jodie felt fine. She really enjoyed just being home—the few times she dared leave Brandy alone and venture downstairs to be with the rest of the family. Davy Golding had even come by to pay a visit. They'd been hot and heavy for all of senior year of high school. He'd married and divorced, "Standard practice for us lawyers," he'd joked with a good laugh. He'd also matured a lot and she wouldn't have minded checking out the possibilities. But there were only so many times she could invite him to her bedroom—that probably smelled a bit too much of dog—to sit in the creaky desk chair and watch her hold Brandy, who cowered at his presence.

Brandy had always been the fun dog: quick to find explosives, glad to pal around with rest of the squad, tolerant of other war dogs, and a total goofball for a Frisbee or her KONG toy. They'd FAST-roped out of Black Hawk helos together, parachuted out of C-130s at thirty thousand feet while both on oxygen, and patrolled through more hellhole towns than she could count.

Not so much fun after the explosion that had given Brandy half of her scars in a split second and had taken out Jodie's right eardrum just for the hell of it.

"You know," Nikita's voice slowed, "Luke mentioned this place once. Somewhere out west. Hang on."

Jodie listened as her friend moved about. She could hear her, leaving the apartment she shared with her SEAL husband Drake, wandering down the barracks hall, and thumping on someone's door. Some whispered conversation of which Jodie could only catch a few words: dog, out west, and that ultimate curse, PTSD.

"This is Commander Luke Altman. Who am I talking to?" His voice was deep and solid as a subway tunnel.

"This is Petty Officer First Class Jodie Jaffe, formerly with SEAL Team—" and her voice choked off.

Luke Altman? Like Mr. Legend SEAL Team 6 Altman? What the hell had Nikita just done to her?

Jodie bolted upright in her bed, heaving the comforter over Brandy. On her feet at full attention, she tried to think of what to say. One didn't talk to such highly decorated officers about such trivia as "my dog is unhappy." Especially not while wearing a Yankee's t-shirt that had been worn thin back in high school, white cotton panties, and not a scrap else.

Brandy shook off the comforter enough to look nervously over at her, but Jodie couldn't make herself move to reassure her.

"What seems to be the problem, petty officer?"

Jodie was going to kill Nikita. But that would have to happen later because it was never good to keep an officer waiting.

"I'm sorry to disturb your evening, sir. I was discussing my dog with Nikita Hayward just now and suddenly I'm on the phone with you. I'm not sure why, sir." Could she sound any stupider?

"Tell me about him."

"Her, sir." Yes, stupider was possible, but she wasn't going down that path to nowhere. So she told him.

She'd been twelve years in, the last six with Brandy inside the SEAL teams—he'd know what a rare honor that was for a woman and just what it said about her and Brandy's competency. Hundreds, maybe thousands of lives saved. Service in the Dust Bowl of Afghanistan as well as Somalia, Yemen, and the unusual list of unmentionables.

"Deep in Syrian battlespace, we caught a bad hit—a mortar, so it wasn't her fault. After a lot of surgery and physical therapy, the vets gave her a clean medical and I did all the paperwork to get her home. But she's suffering badly, sir. Skittish as hell, which isn't like her. She was always rock steady under fire. I'm unsure how to help her."

There was a long silence. She'd spilled it all out in a single rush, the way officers liked their information. Everything relevant, nothing extra around the edges.

The silence stretched long enough that she checked the phone to make sure she still had it against her good ear. She did.

"Hard question first, Jaffe. You up for it?"

"Former SEAL, sir." An enlisted's way of telling an officer they'd asked a dumb-ass question.

"Would putting her down be a kindness?"

"Sir, no sir!" *That* was the kind of advice Nikita had found for her? Like discarding an old weapon? Might as well condone ethnic cleansing while they were at it.

"You willing to do whatever it takes to help her?" Altman moved on before she could say something nasty.

"Sir, yes sir!" She'd already spent two months overseas after her discharge, making sure they didn't put Brandy down before she was pronounced fit for release.

"Got a pen and paper?"

Jodie grabbed the first thing that came to hand, flipped it open, and grabbed a marker pen. "Ready, sir."

He gave her an address. Without realizing, she'd scribbled it across Davy Golding's photo in their old yearbook. Of course it had naturally opened to that page. He'd filled every bit of white space on the page with one of the hottest love letters imaginable—which she might have read more than a few times, so naturally the old yearbook flopped open there. She'd just obliterated whole sections of it with her Sharpie. Jodie wasn't going to read anything into that.

Then she looked at what she'd written across Davy's face and mash note.

"Montana?" She had trouble getting Brandy across the street. Getting her across the country sounded as unlikely as getting the Dodgers back to Brooklyn.

"Just write it down, Jaffe. If anyone can help you, it'll be Stan Corman."

"What're you doing out here on such a fine spring day, Stan?"

"Pissing myself. Go away." He really didn't need Patrick's questions at the moment.

"Sure thing," and Patrick slid down off his horse to come stand beside him. "What are you looking at?"

"At where I pissed myself." At the goddamn limitless

Montana prairie where an unknown load of suckitude was apparently inbound.

Patrick actually leaned forward to look down at the front of Stan's jeans.

Stan swung his left arm into Patrick's gut hard enough to make him grunt—and mostly double over.

Odd. Stan didn't often forget that his left arm was made of metal from the biceps down. "Sorry, buddy. Been a bad start to my day."

"Expecting someone?" Patrick shrugged it off. From this bluff southeast of the ranch house and barns, he could see the first dozen of the thirty miles of dirt road to Choteau—the nearest town.

"Your wife and your mother. We're gonna have a three-way." The Larson cattle ranch spread for eighty thousand acres across the low roll of the Montana plains in a carpet of brilliant spring green. In another month it would be cooked-down brown. That land was a sharp contrast to this spread. Henderson's Ranch started at the dirt-road boundary with Larson's and straddled the more rugged foothills of the Front Range from this bluff, going ten miles back to the sudden upshot of the Rocky Mountains and the Flathead Wilderness.

"She's not my wife—not for two weeks yet. Besides, you try to tangle with Lauren, good luck to you." Patrick leaned back against his horse like it was a barn wall.

"Next you're gonna be plucking a piece of grass to chew so that you and your horse look even more alike."

Patrick did just that and grinned at him. He was wearing that goofy-guy smile. So besotted you couldn't even tease him none.

Stan turned back to watch the horizon. Pa had once said that women were a bottomless pit that men fell into and never recovered. As he hadn't remarried and had barely dated since Ma had run off with some insurance man when Stan was three, meant he probably knew what he was on about.

But Patrick sure looked to be enjoying the fall.

He was just as bad as his brother, the ranch's chef, who'd married the ranch's head cowgirl last fall. Six months and they still looked and acted like the honeymoon would never end. There was enough happy couple shit on this ranch to gag a guy. Just give Stan his training dogs and he was fine.

He and Patrick had shared a bunkroom for three years and all of a sudden Patrick was all Mister Luv. Stan had gotten to like living with Patrick—a naively optimistic goofball who'd also become a better-than-decent cowboy and trail guide. Stan missed him now that he'd moved into one of the cabins with Lauren. Of course she was hot as hell and a former war dog handler, so he cut her some slack for that. Just like him, she'd also lost her dog in combat, which cut her a lifetime's worth of slack. She'd been lucky enough to make it out in one piece herself, but he knew that didn't make the loss any easier. Survivor's guilt probably made it harder in some ways, not that he'd ever ask. The memory of his dog was etched on his skin. And his metal arm.

But what was coming down the road today, he had no fuckin' idea.

His CO—or he had been back when Stan still had

two hands to scratch himself with—had sent him a text just as chatty as ever.

Sending you a dog. Needs help.

He didn't like this shit at all. He raised and trained young dogs for Special Operations units. That was it. He could field-stitch a wounded dog, but he wasn't some veterinarian.

But you couldn't just say no to a man like Commander Altman.

That itch between his shoulder blades had only failed him once. Actually, it had been there—and he'd ignored it. And it was itching now. Last time he'd lost an arm, this time…

So, he had texted it anyway.

Hell no!

Altman had replied, *There within the hour.* Then he'd gone silent.

Asshole. Sometimes the truth just needed to be pointed out.

Still no response. If ST6 commanders used emojis, Stan could feel the smiley slapping into his forehead.

Then, weirdly enough, a smiley did appear. That new wife of Altman's, Zoe something, was definitely a bad influence. Stan had never expected Altman to fall, but he had. If Stan had Patrick's sense of humor, he'd probably be humming "Another One Bites the Dust." He wasn't Patrick. Thank God for small favors.

Altman had invited him to the wedding, but last thing Stan wanted was to hang with his old teammates who would stare at his metal arm like he was a fucking cripple. He already knew that shit and didn't need them to tell him.

That itch had made him to walk up here onto the bluff to watch east for an incoming transport. The only military base in Montana, other than a couple of National Guard units and a whole lot of missile silos, was Malmstrom Air Force Base over in Great Falls, a hundred miles east. So far the only black specs he'd spotted in the sky were a pair of high-circling turkey vultures.

Ain't dead yet, he thought at them. *Come to pick my carcass, you're gonna bust your beak on these steel bones.* Actually his arm was mostly aluminum and titanium, still didn't make him roadkill.

Patrick was talking about the upcoming wedding. Patrick's brother had gotten married last October during the winter's first big storm. Lauren was going to be a June bride. With Montana weather, who knew; there still might be a storm, but not too likely.

"Why'd you wait so long?" He asked to keep Patrick talking, as if Stan didn't already know the story. But he needed the distraction.

"Well, you know that Mom and Dad are professors at Stonybrook University in New York, right? They could only stay for a couple days for Nathan's wedding, but they really liked it out here. I figured if we waited until the semester was over and the weather was nice, they could stay a while and really enjoy themselves. You know that Mom still wants to talk about your arm?"

"Uh-huh." Yeah, like that was gonna happen. She might be some hotshot head of the nation's first-and-foremost biomed engineering school. Didn't mean that he wanted to be some sad-sack guinea pig. "Like my arm just fine the way it is."

"But—"

"Drop it, Patrick."

"Stan, seriously. I think—"

"One thing is damn clear, boy."

"What's that?"

"You were never military."

"Why *this* time?"

"What part of 'drop it' don't you understand?"

"All the parts," Patrick tipped back his cowboy hat to scratch at his forehead in confusion. "Don't you want—"

"Nope."

That finally stopped him.

"Well, it looks like whatever you're waiting for is just about here."

"What? Where?" Stan checked the sky again.

Patrick pointed down at the dirt road winding around the base of the bluff. A black Dodge Ram truck with a dog-sized cage in the back rolled along, raising a long trail of slow-settling dust.

That meant that Altman hadn't texted him until he was turning off Highway 287 onto the road out to the ranch.

Typical.

"Let's go down and meet him," Patrick gathered up his horse's reins and turned to lead the way.

"Altman's an asshole." What kind of a SEAL commander let his wife corrupt him into using emojis?

But Stan was out of options. After the pickup swung out of sight around the base of the bluff and toward the long ranch drive, he turned and followed Patrick leading his horse down to the ranch compound. Place always looked like a picture postcard from up here.

The sprawling log-cabin main house commanded the central yard from its place at the base of the next rise of land. Two long horse barns and the mother of all machinery garages lay across the broad parking area. The ranch manager's smaller house—the main house in miniature—nestled out beyond the barns. His dog kennel and training grounds lay in the low meadow around to the northeast past the bunkhouses for the hands. He'd had to argue with Mac, the ranch owner, so that they were way out of the action. The less he had to do with nosy ranch guests, the happier he was.

The guest cabins climbed the west face of the bluff on the opposite side of the main house, offering a clear view east and south, and well-protected from the chill northerlies that blew down off the Canadian Plains.

Beyond the cabins rolled the hills of the Montana Front Range. In the ten miles that belonged to Henderson's Ranch, the land changed from prairie to the abrupt edge of the Rocky Mountains that etched a rugged line into the Big Sky. He'd fought all over the world and even after three years here, it was still one of the most breathtaking places he'd ever been.

And then the black pickup rolled into the central compound and ground to a halt.

Time to go give Altman a piece of his mind.

Though he wouldn't mind meeting that wife of his—had to be some serious kind of lady to match up right.

Keep reading this completed series at fine retailers everywhere:
Christmas at Henderson's Ranch
Reaching Out at Henderson's Ranch
Nathan's Big Sky
Welcome at Henderson's Ranch
Big Sky, Loyal Heart
Finding Henderson's Ranch
Emily's Christmas Gift
Big Sky Dog Whisperer

ABOUT THE AUTHOR

M.L. Buchman started the first of over 50 novels and even more short stories while flying from South Korea to ride across the Australian Outback. All part of a solo around-the-world bicycle trip (a mid-life crisis on wheels) that ultimately launched his writing career.

Booklist has selected his military and firefighter series(es) as 3-time "Top 10 Romance of the Year." NPR and Barnes & Noble have named other titles "Top 5 Romance of the Year." In 2016 he was a finalist for RWA's RITA award.

He has flown and jumped out of airplanes, can single-hand a fifty-foot sailboat, and has designed and built two houses. In between writing, he also quilts. M.L. is constantly amazed at what can be done with a degree in geophysics. He also writes: contemporary romance, thrillers, and SF. More info at: www.mlbuchman.com

Join the conversation:
www.mlbuchman.com

Other works by M. L. Buchman:

The Night Stalkers
MAIN FLIGHT
The Night Is Mine
I Own the Dawn
Wait Until Dark
Take Over at Midnight
Light Up the Night
Bring On the Dusk
By Break of Day
WHITE HOUSE HOLIDAY
Daniel's Christmas
Frank's Independence Day
Peter's Christmas
Zachary's Christmas
Roy's Independence Day
Damien's Christmas
AND THE NAVY
Christmas at Steel Beach
Christmas at Peleliu Cove
5E
Target of the Heart
Target Lock on Love
Target of Mine

Firehawks
MAIN FLIGHT
Pure Heat
Full Blaze
Hot Point
Flash of Fire
Wild Fire
SMOKEJUMPERS
Wildfire at Dawn
Wildfire at Larch Creek
Wildfire on the Skagit

Delta Force
Target Engaged
Heart Strike
Wild Justice

White House Protection Force
Off the Leash
On Your Mark
In the Weeds

Where Dreams
Where Dreams are Born
Where Dreams Reside
Where Dreams Are of Christmas
Where Dreams Unfold
Where Dreams Are Written

Eagle Cove
Return to Eagle Cove
Recipe for Eagle Cove
Longing for Eagle Cove
Keepsake for Eagle Cove

Henderson's Ranch
Nathan's Big Sky
Big Sky, Loyal Heart

Love Abroad
Heart of the Cotswolds: England
Path of Love: Cinque Terre, Italy

Dead Chef Thrillers
Swap Out!
One Chef!
Two Chef!

Deities Anonymous
Cookbook from Hell: Reheated
Saviors 101

SF/F Titles
The Nara Reaction
Monk's Maze
the Me and Elsie Chronicles

Strategies for Success (NF)
Managing Your Inner Artist/Writer
Estate Planning for Authors

SIGN UP FOR M. L. BUCHMAN'S
NEWSLETTER TODAY

and receive:
Release News
Free Short Stories
a Free Book

Do it today. Do it now.
http://free-book.mlbuchman.com

Printed in Great
Britain
by Amazon